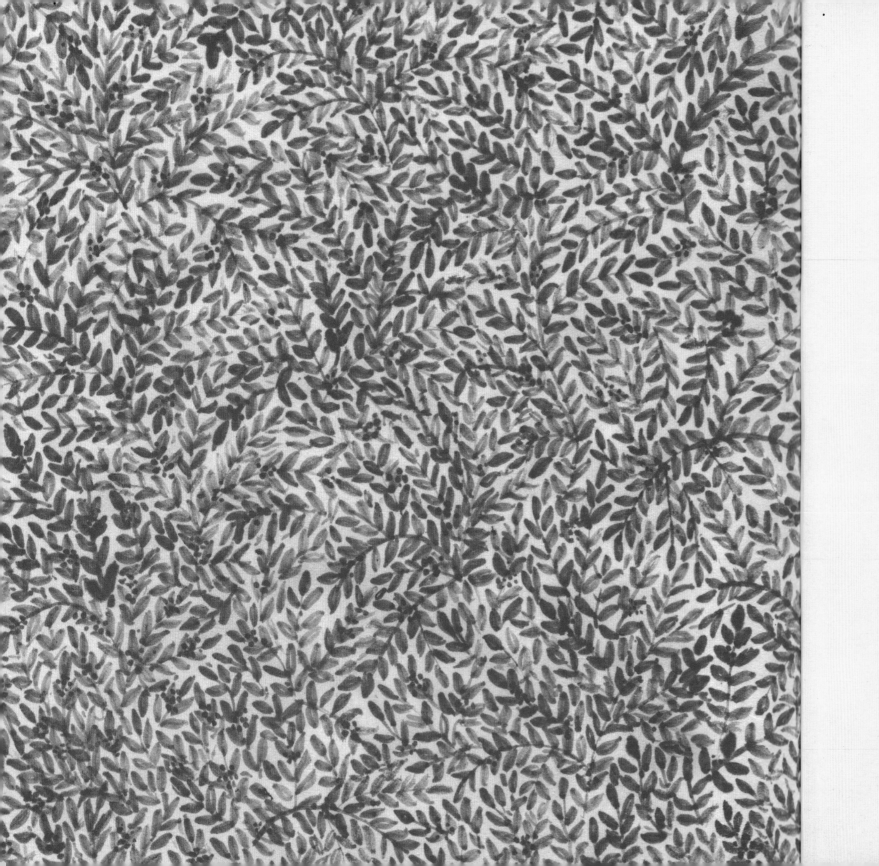

ALSO

E. B. GOODALE

HOUGHTON MIFFLIN HARCOURT
Boston   New York

Today, I am at my gramma's house,
high on the hill,
amongst the blueberry bushes.

And *also* …

. . . I am remembering camping with Mama. Wandering away from our tent—all was quiet except for a rustling in the trees.

Today, my gramma is at the kitchen sink,
watching me from the window.

And *also* . . .

. . . she is remembering being a little girl in her mother's garden. Surprised by a bunny in a bush, she spent the rest of the afternoon in wet shoes.

Today, my mama is walking down the hill, coming to find me.

And *also*...

. . . she is remembering sorting blueberries
in the breakfast nook of her mama's kitchen.
Her sister was making her giggle.

Today, Gramma's cat, Nutmeg, is
next to me, rolling in the grass.

And *also* ...

. . . she is remembering being tiny and hungry,
worrying about her next meal. Until a hand
reached down to rescue her.

Now,
many years have passed,
and I am sitting at my desk
writing this book.

And *also* . . .

. . . I am remembering being a little girl
at my gramma's house,
high on the hill,
amongst the blueberry bushes.

With Gramma at the window,

with Mama coming to find me,

with Nutmeg by my side.

We are all here . . .

. . . and *also* there.

Always.

For Gramma and Papa

BLUEBERRY INK RECIPE:

With the help of an adult, thaw a ½ cup of wild, frozen blueberries.

Mash them gently through a strainer, collecting the juice in a jar.

Add ½ teaspoon salt and ½ teaspoon vinegar and mix thoroughly.

Paint away and watch how the color changes as it dries!

Copyright © 2022 by E. B. Goodale

hmhbooks.com

The illustrations in this book were done on kitakata paper using monoprint, gouache, and blueberry ink.
The text type was set in Bembo Std.
The display text was hand-lettered.

Jacket design by Whitney Leader-Picone
Interior design by Whitney Leader-Picone

The Library of Congress Cataloging-in-Publication Data is on file.

ISBN: 978-0-358-15394-8

Printed in Italy
1
4500836207

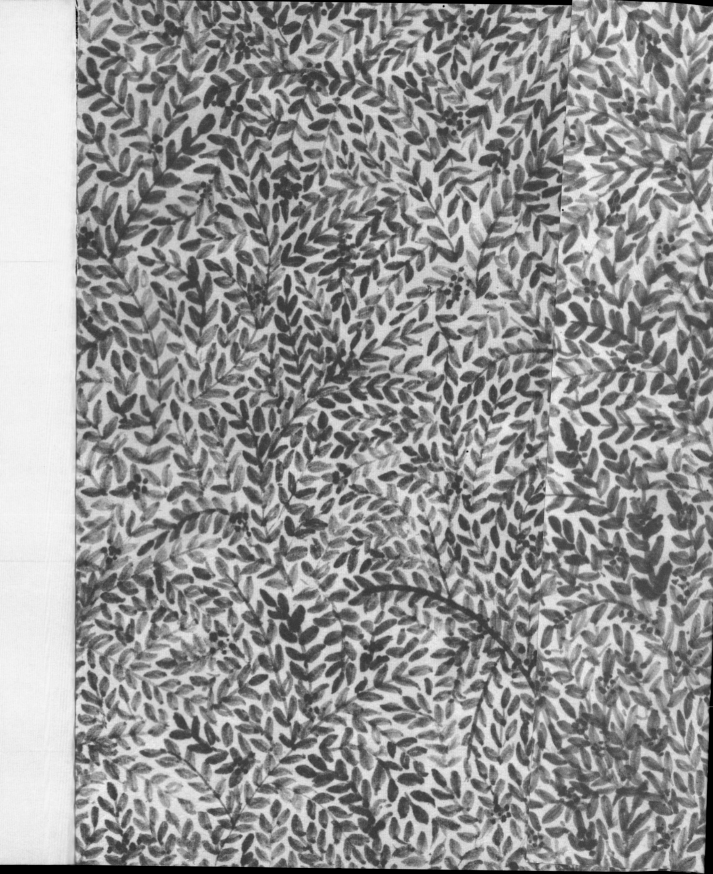